"Big, colorful storytelling with clear gospel messages. Kids plead for just one more."

—SHEREE MACPHERSON, children's ministries leader

"A master storyteller who transports the reader and arouses empathy."

—CATHERINE SMYTHE, retired teacher

The Bull Story &
Other Inspiring Tails

The Bull Story & Other Inspiring Tails

Grenville Kent

RESOURCE *Publications* • Eugene, Oregon

THE BULL STORY AND OTHER INSPIRING TAILS

Resource Publications
An Imprint of Wipf and Stock Publishers
199 W. 8th Ave., Suite 3
Eugene, OR 97401

www.wipfandstock.com

PAPERBACK ISBN: 979-8-3852-2184-4
HARDCOVER ISBN: 979-8-3852-2185-1
EBOOK ISBN: 979-8-3852-2186-8

VERSION NUMBER 06/06/24

For Zizzer, Mars, Moog, T-Bob, Jock and Professor Snoog.
If I paused during a bedtime story, you
would say, "Keep telling!"

For Aleta. The heart of her husband safely trusts in her.

And for Bernadene, my Godmother, who never
lets me forget that tragedy can become comedy
and the One enthroned in heaven will laugh.

These stories are based on actual events,
though I have used some imagination.

Contents

1

The Bull Story

BELSHAZZAR THE BULL WAS 996 kg of muscle and bone, plus a few brain cells. He was well looked after on my grandfather's farm and should have been happy, but he was mean, ornery and threatening.

He had a sensitive pink nose with a copper nose-ring in it. One tug there could really hurt him, so a rope made him behave himself—but only just.

Every few months my grandfather read his children another newspaper report of some poor farm worker dying after a bull gored him with its horns or slammed him up against a fence or stomped him to pulp with its hooves.

They knew how dangerous Belshazzar was, and enjoyed coming up with insults for the big, bad, belligerent, bellicose, bolshie, bumptious boofhead, etc etc.

The cow paddock was a shortcut on their way home from school. Their father warned them often and the sign on the fence was very clear: *Bull In Paddock. Keep Out!*

But you guessed it. One summer afternoon, my father's brother Grenville, aged eleven, saw the paddock was empty. The cows were being milked and there was no sign of Belshazzar. He must have been off servicing someone else's herd, earning money for the farm.

Gren jumped over the barbed wire fence. He took another careful look around. The sign was wrong and he was right. No bull.

He took a few more steps, still looking and listening.

And of course it was when he was near the middle of the paddock that he heard heavy footsteps and turned around to see the bovine bully boy come out from behind a tree, put his head down and charge.

Gren was already running like his life depended on it. And it did.

Belshazzar's top speed was about 60 km/h (compared with 43.99 kilometers per hour for Usain Bolt).

Gren knew he was being chased by something that weighed as much as a car and moved just as fast, but he thought he just might have one small advantage. He may be more maneuverable.

Far too soon he heard the hoofsteps gaining on him. He could hear Belshazzar puffing right behind him, and feel his breath on his neck. Its smelt like a compost heap.

At the last second, Gren faked to his right and stepped hard left.

Belshazzar wasn't expecting that. His momentum kept him going straight ahead but with lightning reflexes he flicked his head left to stab a horn into Gren's rib cage and puncture his lung, making him unable to run anymore. But he missed by a whisker.

He kept trundling forward for a second, but the big fella was surprisingly nimble. He turned his huge carcass around, skidding and throwing out divots of grass, and was about to accelerate until Gren lifted his hands high in the air and shook them around, shouting, *"Buddada-boodadda-buddada! Booddada-buddada-biddada-boddada-booddada!"*

Belshazzar was shocked. For a vital second, he stopped dead, trying to think this through. *Huh? Where has that boy gone? What is this big, loud monster?*

Gren legged it again, straight for the nearest fence.

It took Belshazzar's brain cells a second to think. *It's not a monster. It's a boy. Attack!* It took him another second to get going again.

Gren felt he might have a chance. He had a slight lead now. But it wouldn't be enough.

Much sooner than he expected, he heard and smelt Belshazzar right behind him again. This time Gren stepped off his left foot and went hard right. Belshazzar was expecting something like that and he speared his right horn with deadly accuracy at the exact spot where Gren's body was. Luckily Gren had dropped to the ground and rolled, and the horn sliced the air above his head.

Again the bull overshot with more than five hundred hamburgers of weight, but again he U-turned quickly and was about to charge towards. . . a monster that was very wide and high and making a loud, shocking noise. *Murpala-moopala-murpala-moopala! Moppidy-doppity!*

Belshazzar stopped again and turned his head on its side to get another look. *Huh? No, it's just a boy. Oh. And he's getting away.* He started pumping his legs again and was soon up to full speed.

A third time Gren heard the deadly rumble of hooves right behind him but he couldn't yet smell the breath and he saw the barbed wire fence only a few meters away. He knew he would be head-butted in the backside any second and sent flying into the air. He braced for the terrible pain as a horn tore into the muscle of his thigh and brought him down, and huge hooves trampled him to death so close but so far from home.

But he jumped anyway, the biggest hurdle of his life, and he was hit from behind by nothing at all and felt nothing but elation and relief as he flew over the fence and landed in a blackberry patch. Phew! A few thorn scratches were nothing compared with what could have happened.

Belshazzar skidded to a halt with his delicate pink nose only millimeters from the barbed wire. He snorted and glared at Gren. *Try that again!*

After that, Gren walked the long way round. Every time.

He didn't tell his parents what had happened, but somehow his father knew. That night he said, "Gren, I don't need to punish you for disobedience. Belshazzar has done that. But after a foolish and almost deadly decision, you stayed calm and kept your courage and you survived. Well done, my boy. We would have missed you very much." Gren thought he saw a small tear shining in the corner of his father's eye.

People make mistakes and do sins, and some people talk like God hates us for that, but I've read better news in the Bible. God always loves all his children. All of his advice is for our benefit. When we don't listen, and we hurt ourselves or others, God knows a good scare can be quite educational but he never wants us damaged. He wants us to recover quickly, make amends to people as much as we can and get back on track. In fact He's dying for that to happen—that's the gospel truth.

"I don't enjoy seeing anyone die," says God. "So turn around and live" (Ezek 18:32).

I love that about God.

2

The Polish Pilot

WHEN HIS AIRCRAFT ENGINE began sounding the wrong note, Roman Turski knew he had to land straightaway.

The nearest airport would be Vienna, but it had just been taken over by the Nazis. Roman wanted to stay right away from Nazis. He expected they would invade his home country of Poland next, and that was why he was flying home to join the Polish Air Force, having quit his job as a flight instructor in France.

But landing in Nazi Vienna would not be as dangerous as a breakdown in his one engine, so he landed the little plane. The hangar mechanics said they would do the repairs overnight, and Roman went to find a hotel.

Swastika flags hung from nearly every building. Soldiers in grey were everywhere, and Roman saw some of the black uniforms of the Gestapo, Hitler's secret police. He couldn't wait to leave the next day.

As he walked around Vienna, Roman didn't see any sign of Jewish shops or buildings. That made him happy. He had joined anti-Jewish protest marches back home, hoping to push the Jews out of Poland. He and his friends had picked on Jews in the streets, mocking their beards and hats, and he had often thrown stones through the windows of Jewish shops. He knew his Christian father was appalled by that behavior, but he thought his father was old-fashioned. That was the one good thing about the Nazis, Roman thought. They got rid of the Jews.

Before checking out of his hotel next morning, Roman went out to buy some souvenirs. As he stepped out the front door, a man ran smack into him and nearly knocked him over. Roman grabbed him by the shirt and was ready to throw a punch when he saw the man's thin face was pale with fear. "Gestapo!" he said. "Gestapo!" He was puffing and wriggling to escape Roman's grip.

My enemy's enemy is my friend, Roman thought in a flash. If the Gestapo are after this man, then I'm on his side.

Roman pulled the man up to his feet and gestured for him to follow. They walked casually back through the hotel lobby and ran up the stairs. Roman unlocked his room and looked around. Under the bed? In the wardrobe? The bath? Too obvious. Roman had a moment of fear: "What have I done, risking my life for this stranger?"

The man was quite small, so Roman lifted the covers of his bed and pointed. The man lay down and bent his body into an L-shape. Roman carefully arranged the sheets and blankets so the bed looked messy and unmade. He took off his clothes and lay them on the bed so he could pretend he had just woken up. He lathered his face with soap and took out his razor.

Soon he heard heavy boots clomping up the stairs. There was a shout in German and a fist banged on his door.

Roman opened up and Gestapo officers pushed into the room shouting questions at him. He said, "*Ich verstehe nicht.*" He really didn't understand. They searched under the bed, in the wardrobe and in the bath. They demanded his passport but gave it back and left. Soon he heard them knocking next door.

Roman let a few minutes pass, then lifted the bedclothes and the little man rolled out with a huge smile on his face.

They didn't speak the same language, so Roman held his arms out like wings, then took out his flight maps. The man pointed to the city of Warsaw in Poland. Roman shook his head and pointed to a green country area near Krakow. The man nodded. Roman drew police on the corner of the map. The man nodded and his dark eyes beamed with thanks.

At the airport, Roman told the Nazi customs and immigration officers that his friend just wanted to see him off, so they let them walk out to the aircraft together. At the last minute the little man jumped in and Roman gunned the engine. What could those Nazis do? Soon Vienna looked like a toy city below and behind them.

They crossed Czechoslovakia and saw the Vistula River shining below, and a railway line.

As the little aircraft landed in Krakow, armed police were waiting for it. "You helped a wanted man escape from Vienna," they said.

"Me?" Roman laughed.

"We have a warrant to search your plane."

"Go ahead."

Roman had already put the man down on some farmer's field not far from a railway station and given him a map and most of his money. He remembered the look in the man's dark eyes as he shook his hand, turned and walked into the woods.

The Krakow police found nothing and had to let Roman go.

"By the way, what was your escapee wanted for?" he asked.

"He was a Jew."

＊　＊

Soon the Nazis unleashed Blitzkrieg on Poland. They had vastly greater numbers and newer technology, but the tiny Polish Air Force managed to shoot down one hundred and seventy planes of Hitler's Luftwaffe. Roman was one of the brave pilots who fought against overwhelming odds. When the war was lost, many pilots fled to France to continue their fight for freedom. Roman tried to escape via Romania, but was caught and sent to a concentration camp.

After a hellish time there, he managed to escape and join the French Air Force, aiming once again to stop Hitler. When France surrendered, he flew across the Channel to England.

He joined the Royal Air Force, as did many superb Polish pilots. The Luftwaffe still had vastly more aircraft than the RAF, and Roman said, "Our only superiority was morale."

During the Battle of Britain, death rained down on the people of London night after night from the bellies of Heinkel and Dornier bombers that droned overhead with Messerschmitt fighters in support. Brave men in Hurricanes and Spitfires risked their lives to protect the men, women and children below. Two Polish fighter squadrons were among the best in the RAF.

The Nazis tried with all their might to break the British spirit. It is no exaggeration to say that the fate of Western civilization hung on that battle in the skies of Britain, and that pilots like Roman saved the day. Winston Churchill famously spoke of airmen "who, undaunted by odds, unweakened by their constant challenge and mortal danger, are turning the tide of world war by their prowess and devotion. Never in the field of human conflict has so much been owed by so many to so few."

As the tide of war turned, the RAF could begin counterattacking. Roman and the "few" began attacking Nazi airfields in France.

On a raid near Boulogne, Roman shot down five enemy fighters, which was a record. On the way home he had a sixth Messerschmitt lined up in his gunsights. He stabbed the fire button but heard only the hiss of compressed air. He had used up all his bullets. He decided the fighter wasn't getting away to kill again, so he rammed his plane into it.

As his propellor chewed away its tailplane, a piece of metal sheared off, spun through the air and sliced through the windscreen of Roman's Spitfire, slashing deep into his forehead. He could feel warm blood pouring down his face and neck. He began feeling faint from the pain and the blood loss, but he had to get himself back across the English Channel and land his plane. A friend saw he was in trouble and flew right beside him, shouting over the radio to keep him awake, but as Roman crossed the English coastline, he blacked out.

And that, as his English friends used to say, was that.

❦ ❧

He felt himself coming back to life in a beautiful place where everything was peaceful and calm, and kind people with beautiful faces and white clothes spoke to him, caring about his every need.

He felt disappointed to have died, but happy he had made it to heaven.

An angel in white brought him something sweet to drink and he decided to have a nice relaxing sleep for a little longer.

He woke to see a face smiling at him. "Do you remember me?"

Thin face, dark eyes, speaking English with a German accent . . . No, Roman didn't remember.

"You saved my life in Vienna."

"Did I? Ah, yes. How did you die?"

"What?" said the man, smiling.

"How did you die?" asked Roman quite seriously. He wondered why they had let a Jew into heaven, but he didn't say that out loud.

"Ah, it's a long story," said the man, his dark eyes sparkling. "When you dropped me near Krakow, an old friend helped me to escape just before the Nazis invaded. I came to Scotland and began work. When one of the Polish squadrons did famously well in the Battle of Britain, I thought you might be in it. I checked with the Royal Air Force and indeed you were."

"Hmm."

"And yesterday I read in the paper that a top Polish ace had shot down five enemy aircraft in one day! I was delighted, but they also said he was seriously injured after stopping a sixth attacker and crash-landing his plane."

"Did I crash-land? I don't remember. . ."

"Yes, your friend reported seeing your head flopped over in the cockpit, so he thinks you were unconscious when you crash-landed on farmland." The man smiled. "So it seems you can even fly in your sleep."

Roman grinned.

"Anyway, the newspaper said you were not expected to survive. So I immediately asked the Air Force to fly me urgently down here from Scotland to this hospital."

"We're in a hospital?"

"Yes, this is a hospital. We're not in heaven yet, sorry. When I arrived, the chief surgeon indicated a severely fractured skull. He had decided you were so near to death that it would be a waste of time and resources to operate."

"Then how. . .?"

"I convinced him otherwise. I thought at last I could do something to thank you for saving my life. I operated on you this morning. You see, I am a brain surgeon. You are going to recover well."

Roman Turski lived to fight another day. He later wrote a book called *The Evaders*, and said that through all this he learned that he should obey the Bible's command to:

"Love your neighbor as yourself"

-Moses (Lev 19:18), quoted by Jesus (Mark 12:31) as the second-greatest commandment.

3

Bumpy

Roy was smiling sleepily in the soft morning sunshine as he walked down his driveway—and was shocked out of his brain by noise.

BARARARARARARARAAAA!

He jumped and his whole body tensed for fight or flight. It seemed the neighbors had a new dog.

It was trying to break free from its chain, and barking with eardrum-popping aggression at Roy. It was a German Shepherd, but was an angry red color, as if a Red Setter had snuck into its ancestry. The fur on its back stood up in a funny way that earned it the name Bumpy.

Grumpy more like, Roy thought as every day he was barked at in his own yard by a mutt that obviously wanted to lick up his bone marrow. Clearly it loved its neighbors as protein.

"Nice boy," said Roy hopefully. "There's a good dog." But day after day, week after week, his ears were assaulted in his own yard. And Roy worried what might happen to his wife and children if the dog ever broke its chain.

Then one day Roy noticed the bark was quieter. He looked over to see Bumpy moving slowly. His water bowl was empty and it was a hot day. He didn't seem to have food either. Roy remembered his neighbors had gone away on a month's holidays. They would have arranged someone to care for their dog, but maybe the person wasn't bothering.

This was Roy's chance to get rid of a really annoying enemy by doing nothing. But he thought of three old words, perhaps the most difficult words ever: love your enemies. He decided that applied to dogs.

Bumpy was lying down, panting pathetically.

Roy hopped the fence and filled his water bowl, pushing it near him with a long stick, just to be safe.

Bumpy slurped the water down in a few seconds and looked gratefully up at Roy, who refilled his bowl.

Roy ran back to his house, rummaged in the pantry and found the best food he had—a tin of spaghetti. He filled the food bowl and pushed it within range. Slurp. Gone. Big brown doggy eyes looked up pleadingly at Roy, so he went home and found another tin. This time he walked right up to Bumpy and filled his bowl without fear. He even gave him a pat.

Bumpy looked a lot better, especially when Roy went and bought dog food.

Bumpy's behavior changed completely, so that Roy took him on walks and even let him play with his children.

It was easier to look after him at Roy's place, and the whole family got involved in caring for him.

A few weeks later the neighbors came back from holidays. They said a huge thank-you to Roy, and only wished he had known about their cat.

Then they took their dog home. Roy's whole family were surprised by how much they missed their woofy friend.

Three minutes later Roy heard a loud scraping noise. He opened his front door and there was Bumpy, his paw scratching at the fly screen door. He was panting and smiling up at Roy. *I made it back!*

Roy was happy to see him, but he had to return him to his owners. He suggested they chain him up.

Three minutes later—*scratch scratch scratch!* Roy went out to see Bumpy with part of a broken chain trailing behind him, looking pleased with himself.

He returned him once again, suggesting that they buy a thicker chain.

That one took Bumpy five minutes. *Scratch scratch scratch!*

Roy returned him yet again, and said, "Can I suggest you go to the hardware store, buy a really thick chain and a metal post. And maybe a metal-backed collar. Just until Bumpy remembers where he lives."

They did. Roy helped them hammer the metal post a meter into the ground.

Roy went home. After fifteen minutes he thought the hardware must have beaten Bumpy. Then *scratch scratch scratch!* Roy went to his door and there was Bumpy with his metal-reinforced collar trailing a huge chain that could have held an aircraft carrier, a strand of fence wire tangled in the chain, and a metal post bent out of shape with a meter of dirt on one end. He was wagging his whole body and obviously feeling like a very clever boy.

The neighbors said, "Look, he has bad memories here and he obviously loves you. Would you like to keep him?"

Roy tried to cover his boyish excitement. "Oh, I guess so," he said.

And so Bumpy the red attack dog and former enemy joined the family.

His love and loyalty included Roy, his wife Lorna and their son and daughter. When the children were out playing, Bumpy would seem to be asleep under a nearby tree but one ear was always tracking them like the radar dish on a navy ship. You might think his eyes were closed, but one eye was always blinking for surveillance.

As his children walked to school in Port Moresby, Papua New Guinea, Roy was glad to know they had a hairy guardian angel.

Once a school bully started shouting and pointing at Roy's son. His four-legged bodyguard appeared silently behind him and growled a bit. The bully didn't stop, so Bumpy gently wrapped his jaws around his wrist, not biting or drawing any blood but leaving no doubt that he could. The tough guy was suddenly very polite.

One night Roy came home late from working and heard a frightened male voice from up above him somewhere, "Sir, dog belong you take-im lap-lap belong me."

Roy looked up one of the trees in his front yard and saw a man. A naked man. His traditional loincloth was lying on the ground below and had some tooth-marks in its front flap, suggesting a narrow escape.

Roy held Bumpy's collar and said, "Alright, come down."

The naked man climbed down the tree (carefully) and Roy said, "I don't know you. Why are you at my house?"

"I wanted to meet you," said the man, looking as dodgy as a three-dollar bill.

"Put your clothes on and we'll go to the police station."

The man tried to run away until Roy asked, "Shall I let my dog go?" He stopped and came back.

The police were happy to see the man. They knew him well as a *rascal-boy* and violent housebreaker, and they locked him up.

Roy often went away by boat for weeks at a time, managing schools and medical clinics and teaching farming skills and Christianity across the country. The first time Bumpy saw him go, he followed him to the dock, looking glum. He grabbed Roy by the cuff of his shirt and tried to pull him back home, moaning sadly. Roy patted him but said no. Then when Roy was busy loading gear, Bumpy snuck onto the boat and tried to stow away in a lifeboat. Roy found him and said, "Go home, you dear old boy, and keep the family safe."

Bumpy dragged himself away looking lugubrious, but he cheered up, went home to Lorna and the children, and never left them alone for weeks.

Then one day he simply disappeared. Lorna had no idea where he may have gone until she happened to drive past the harbor. There on the dock was Bumpy, looking out to sea.

She told him to come home but he refused to obey or even look at her.

At about 10 pm that night, Roy's boat pulled in. No one really knows how Bumpy knew his master was coming home when no one else in the family knew.

Lorna said he did that every time Roy came back from work trips, and she had no idea how it was even possible.

Lorna told me, "See how kindness can turn enemies into friends? That's what God does, hoping that people who ignore him or reject him will understand what he's really like, and come to trust him so he can help them."

She got that idea from Bible: "In the life of Jesus, God was working to bring the whole world back to Himself, not holding their sins against them. That's the great news he has given us" (2 Cor 5:19).

So whatever our past mistakes, we can be friends with God.

4

The Pool of Unspeakable Slime

"Pong, that stinks!" said Hamilton, as he and his friends walked near the waste pool of the local hospital.

"All the toilets flow into that pool," said one boy.

"And all the blood and guts from operations," said another. "And the pus."

"My uncle Cecil had his appendix out," said another. "It would be in there."

"My neighbor drank so much whiskey that he got gout and they had to chop his leg off. I bet it's kicking around in there."

They walked even closer, holding their noses, and saw a pipe running right across the cesspool.

"I dare you," said someone.

Hamilton said nothing. He climbed the fence and stepped up onto the pipe.

The pipe wobbled a bit but held his weight. He took a step. Another.

But when he had made it to the middle... nothing happened. A few more steps and he was safe on the other side. He smiled at his mates. They looked a bit disappointed.

"Bet you can't do it backwards."

Hamilton spun around and took a few steps, but he wasn't wearing sports shoes. He was wearing his best leather shoes and church clothes, because his friends had come to his home for lunch after church and they had all popped out for a quick walk while his mother prepared dessert.

One shoe slipped.

Hamilton windmilled his arms, attempting to recover his balance. He couldn't.

He crouched down and hugged the pipe to avoid falling in. His legs swung below him. One shoe brushed the surface of the pool. A hideous pong came up and his toes felt wet.

Hamilton tried to swing his legs up and over, but this put pressure on his hands and he saw too late that the pipe had green algae growing on it. His hands slipped. He gripped on with his ankles, his face swinging just inches from the watery hell. He tried to swing his arms up and grip on but his ankles slipped off.

He went in nose first.

He felt bubbles and froth on his chin and neck, and his face pushed through a layer of slime as he shot down through the warm, lumpy water. It was dark down there, since sunlight couldn't penetrate. He turned around, held his breath and kicked, imagining another leg in there kicking around with him. *Aargh!*

He swam up until his face broke through the slime layer again, and he could wave the froth apart with his arms and take a breath.

He breast-stroked through floating things he didn't want to think about. He made it to the rough concrete side wall and heaved himself out, trying not to slip on more algae.

His friends stared in silent horror at the bog monster emerging from the muck, inches of thick gloop on its head, something green in its ear, brown stains on its shirt, a birthday cake-sized wodge of crud on its back—and a purple blob that might have been Uncle Cecil's appendix.

"You could die!" one friend encouraged him. "The germs in there. . ."

"What will you do? Your mother won't let you back in the house!"

"She'll chuck you in the bin," said a loyal mate.

"Run to the hospital!"

A thick curd slid off his back and fell onto his heels as he ran home.

He didn't knock on the clean white front door or put even one oozing shoe on the porch. He stood on the lawn and called out without opening his lips. "Mmmmummm!"

He knew his lady mother would be chatting happily with her friends as they added mango, strawberries, raspberries, blueberries and passionfruit to a big creamy pavlova. But Hamilton would never taste pavlova again. Never hug his parents again. He would be banished.

"Nnndadnn!"

He knew his dad would be talking with his friends while they washed up.

"Mmmummm!"

His mother thought she heard something and walked to the front door to check. It opened to reveal a swamp beast dripping feculent filth on her neatly trimmed lawn. Her hand went to her nose and her face wrinkled with shock.

"Mmmummm!" said the beast.

"Hamilton?"

The beast mumbled something through a closed mouth.

"Come round to the back lawn, dear," she said, very, very calmly.

His dad came out the back door and said, "Oh, you poor old soldier. Let's get you clean." He hosed him down, leaving a pile of malodorous clart on the garden. The plants would grow extra well there that season. (Thanks, Uncle Cecil.)

"Alright, let's have your duds off," said his dad. Hamilton stripped to his underpants and his dad hosed him again.

His mum had laid a trail of old towels to the bathroom. Hamilton followed them and slid into warm, clean water that was singing with disinfectant. He lay there until a filthy ring formed around the tub. His mum got him out for a minute, wiped away the ring and ran a fresh bath. Then he soaked again.

She scrubbed inside his ears and made him gargle Dettol. When she was satisfied, she brought his clothes and said, "Alright, my dear, you can get dressed."

As he was changing, his dad called through the door, "Come on, old son. Your friends are starving for dessert."

Dessert!

His mum never said a word about his fall. His dad even cut him a second helping of pavlova. Why? Love, of course.

Hamilton told me, "My father and mother acted like Jesus, who 'loved us and washed us from our sins' (Rev 1:5)."

❧   ❧

Hamilton didn't die of some mutant infection from the hospital cesspool. He grew up and became a surgeon who worked in hospitals in poor areas of the Pacific islands. On weekends he travelled with his family to tell people the good news about the love and grace of Jesus. Doctor Lynn Hamilton McMahon was my uncle.

5

He Fought the Law

MARTIN STOLE THE HANG glider while its owner was in the bathroom. He strapped it on, ran to the nearby cliff and jumped off.

I shouted for him to stop and not be an idiot, but he ignored me. We were friends who often spent school lunchtimes reading about flight—books about the first aviators, reports of space missions, or articles about Californian hippies strapping homemade flying machines to their backs and jumping off the Rockies. Clearly Martin had paid attention.

The glider pilot came back and bellowed, "Where's my kite?"

I pointed out to sea.

"What?! Who?"

"Um. . ." I explained.

"Do you know him? Tell me he's an experienced pilot at least."

"He's a schoolboy. He's never flown," I said.

As the pilot cursed, I added, "But he's read a lot about it." That didn't seem to help.

There was nothing either of us could do but watch Martin soaring above Sydney Harbor. He was obviously practicing. He made a slightly shaky turn to the right, then straightened up, then turned left. He seemed to be getting the hang of gliding.

Then he stopped in mid-air. It was like in the Road Runner cartoons when the Wily Coyote runs off a cliff and just hangs in the air for a while until he looks down.

We wondered how Martin could just stop like that. It turned out he had hit the top of a yacht mast. He hung there for a while until the fabric split, the mast pushed through and Martin fell to the deck with a thud.

The yachtsman was not happy. He ranted and swore so much that Martin unstrapped the glider harness and dived overboard, swimming back a couple of hundred meters to the shore to avoid being thumped—or hit with the damage bill.

But we were there on our school picnic and the pilot told the school, so Martin's father heard about it. Martin had to work in the holidays to pay back every cent to the glider pilot and the yachtie.

♦   ♦

A few years later Martin built his own glider out of aluminum tubing, plastic sheets and lots of gaffer tape. He copied the plans from *Scientific American* but decided to double the dimensions. He called it The Vulture.

On his first trial down a mild slope in a gentle wind, a gust caught The Vulture and flung it backwards about fifty meters into a grove of trees. I found Martin there, hanging upside down in his harness. I hoped he was still alive. "Great lift-to-weight ratio," he grinned.

In those summer holidays I helped him off fences, off his back and out of the farm dam. I admired his determination but never ever felt the slightest need to try it myself.

♦   ♦

Martin stayed alive. He grew up—at least in height.

Recently I visited his riverside home and his wife answered the door. We chatted for a while and she said, "If you're looking for Martin. . ." and just pointed upwards.

We went out onto the balcony and there was the Birdman of Berowra, high above the river in his latest ultralight with landing floats. He waved and cut the engine, and for a magic moment the little craft glided down in total silence with the setting sun glowing behind it. It swooshed down onto the sparkling surface like a pelican.

Martin still had the same silly grin on his face as when he stole the glider. Clearly he still loved defying the law of gravity using the laws of aerodynamics.

You don't need me to tell you that another law of gravity operates in human minds, trying to smash our lives on the rocks: "The wrong things we desire are pretty obvious—porn, cheating in marriage, sex without love or commitment, idol-worship, witchcraft, hatred, making trouble, fighting, jealousy, outbursts of rage, selfishness, stirring up conflict, envy, drunkenness, reckless partying and other sins like these. I need to warn you again: people who do these things are not in God's kingdom" (Gal 5:19–21).

But there's another law lifting us: "The fruits of the Spirit are love, joy, peace, patience, kindness, goodness, faithfulness, gentleness and self-control" (Gal 5:22–23).

If we're aware—not numbed by addictions or convenient lies—then we can feel both these laws working on us at once. The trick is to keep choosing the good one, asking God to be the wind beneath our wings.

"In Jesus, the law of the life-giving Spirit sets you free from the law of sin and death" (Rom 8:2).

6

I'd Love A Drink

TONY KNEW SOMETHING WAS wrong.

He and his wife Lee were enjoying a holiday in Canberra. Their son Sam, seventeen, had stayed home in Blacksmiths Beach near Newcastle, but he wasn't returning calls.

Sam had been out with friends on Saturday night, but no one had heard from him since. He had arranged to meet his girlfriend at lunchtime on Sunday, but he hadn't arrived.

"Teenagers," everyone said.

But Tony knew Sam wasn't like that. He was reliable and open with his parents. So where on earth was he? Tony left messages and called all Sam's friends, but by Sunday night, Tony and Lee were worried enough to jump into their car and drive the five hours back to their home, interrupting their holiday.

They got home at 1:30 am on Monday, and Tony went straight to the police station.

The officers on night duty were not worried. They said teenagers could run away or lose their phones, or make plans last minute and forget to tell anyone, or get drunk and sleep all day.

Tony said, "That's not Sam. That would be out of character for him."

The police put out search bulletins and advised Tony to go home and wait.

Tony went home but couldn't sleep. He understood the police saw this kind of thing all the time, but he had an intuition about it.

Lying awake in bed, he remembered a news story from a few years before. A man had driven off the road into a gully where the bushland was so thick that the wreck couldn't be seen from the road. He had not been found for five days and had died. That happened at Crangan Bay on the Pacific Highway, and Sam would have driven through that same area after dropping his friend home.

Tony jumped out of bed, collected all the money he could find, and drove to little Lake Macquarie Airport. He saw a helicopter there and found the office of Skyline Aviation. Their pilot, Lee Mitchell, arrived at work to see a tired, stressed-looking man at the door.

"Mate, I need a helicopter bad. I need to search for my son who might've crashed his car in the bushland near Crangan Bay. I've got $1000 cash. Will that be enough?"

"Sure," Lee said, even though his hourly rate was well above that. "We can start right away." There were high winds that morning, and he had cancelled all his training flights.

"Great, thanks. But I get really airsick. Can I get my brother to fly with you instead?"

"Sure."

While Lee's crew readied the chopper, Tony drove to pick up his brother Michael. Minutes later Lee lifted off with Michael in the passenger seat. Tony was already driving to Crangan Bay.

It took less than ten minutes for Michael to spot a car that looked like Sam's. It was only about twenty meters off the Pacific Highway, but almost totally covered by thick bush. He called Emergency Services, and they started speeding to Crangan Bay with sirens on.

Next Michael phoned Tony, who was ecstatic to hear that news. But Michael also had to say that he couldn't see anyone moving inside. Both brothers were devastated at that news. How would they cope with Sam's death?

The chopper put Michael down on the road, then went and hovered over the crashed car to mark the spot. There was no other way to find it in bushland that thick.

Michael didn't want to go down and look, afraid of what he would find.

He fought his way down the hill through the scrub, calling out Sam's name.

There was no response.

Michael was frantic. The closer he got, the more terrified he felt about finding his nephew's lifeless body.

When he was only steps away, he saw Sam's head moving in the wrecked car. Beside himself with happiness, he texted Tony, "He's alive."

He gave the thumbs up to Lee, who was still hovering above so the Emergency Services crew could quickly find the spot.

When Tony arrived, he ran down the hill to his son's wrecked car and held him. "Mate, Dad's got you," he said.

Sam could only say in a husky voice, "I'd love a drink."

He was seriously dehydrated after a hot summer day that had turned his car into an oven. Tony had the enormous pleasure of giving his son a drink of water.

Tony saw Sam's thigh bone was broken and poking out of a large wound. His arm was broken, his elbow was dislocated, and he had other fractures as well.

Even more serious, he was pinned under the dash from his waist down. Emergency Services had to get their Jaws of Life equipment into a very difficult spot, removing trees to make way for it. They had to peel the roof off the car and cut out seats to pull Sam from the wreckage. It was a very slow and difficult rescue, but Sam had medical care the whole time.

Sam had been there for thirty hours, and an emergency doctor said he wouldn't have lasted much longer.

The worked out that Sam's car had hit a concrete pole at around 80km/h, ripped the driver's door off, slipped down the steep slope beside the road and somehow landed back on its wheels.

Nowadays Sam is getting on with his life and Tony and Lee are glad that they didn't wait.

However much our lives may go off track at times, it encourages me to know that a kind Father always looks for us and will never quit or spare any cost until our rescue is complete. Jesus told a story about a father like that to show people what God was like (Luke 15:11–32).

7

Dadda! Car!

THERE ARE SOME EXPERIENCES you never get over.

Like backing your Toyota out of the garage, hearing a baby scream, and realizing the crunch you are feeling under your wheels is his little bones. Driving forwards off his body, running to the back of the car, and seeing Marcus, my sixteen-month-old son, crushed and dying in a widening pool of blood, holding out his little hands to his dad to help him and, oh dear God, I couldn't help him. . .

Then I woke up.

I looked around and realized it was just a nightmare. I was in my bedroom and the clock was glowing 3:19 am in red digits. Reality had never looked better.

With tears of relief rolling down my cheeks, and puffing as if I had sprinted a hundred meters, I silently thanked God and asked for care and protection for my family. Eventually my breathing slowed and I drifted back to sleep.

I woke up a bit late and had a quick breakfast, thinking about the talk I had to give that morning at church. I didn't even remember my dream.

I needed to load the children into the car. Our garage was crowded with bookshelves and the car door couldn't fully open, so I always backed the car out first.

I checked four-year-old Zoe was with her mother, and I put Marcus by his toys in the dining room, walked through the door into the garage and locked it after me.

When I had the car in reverse, handbrake off, and was about to move my foot from the brake to the accelerator, something felt somehow so familiar that it stopped me. This scene. . . Where had I seen it before? And I remembered my dream. Some of the emotion hit me again, but I reasoned that Marcus was safe—I had locked him into the dining room not even half a minute before. I checked all three mirrors just in case, and turned my head to check the back window. No one. I needed to step on it or I'd be late.

Yet still I sat there arguing with myself, wanting to take my foot off the brake and onto the accelerator, yet feeling uneasy. Was my dream from God? Or just a father's over-active imagination? I looked at the clock in frustration. *Aargh, you'll be late, you sentimental nong.* But I pulled on the handbrake, selected park, and got out of the car, grumbling at myself.

And there, behind the rear offside wheel, was my little boy. He was playing with Bear and his red car. He saw me and shouted excitedly, "Dadda! Car! Car!"

How on earth did he get there? Through a closed internal door, across the lounge-room, out through the snibbed front door and the closed screen door, across the stone front porch with its uneven surfaces, then he must have dropped down to a crawl to duck under the opening automatic garage door without me seeing him.

We didn't know he could reach those door handles, and had never seen him cross the lounge room without help, let alone pull off that long Houdini routine—and all in less than a minute.

What do you do when you haven't killed your son? It's hard for one body to contain that mix of emotions. I scooped him up for a hug, though he wasn't the one who needed it. I'm not sure I was breathing. I clipped him into his seat and went on as though everything was normal, which it wasn't. My feelings were all over the place. I said a thank-you to God which felt strangely mechanical. I went in and found his sister and clipped her into her car seat, sneaking in an extra cuddle on the way.

When his mother joined us, some part of my brain told her what had nearly happened while most of me listened in to someone else's story and was shocked by it. I was emotionally numb—a classic coping mechanism. I managed to tell the people about it in church, but it still felt like a story from a book.

That afternoon I phoned my friend Marcus and told him what had nearly happened to the son named after him. I said, "I respect you're an atheist, but how is this not a miracle? What are the holes in my logic? OK, we all have dreams as our subconscious tidies the filing system in our mind at night, but what are the odds of me having this dream on this night?"

He was blown away and couldn't explain it.

I tried to explain to him that I'm careful about miracle claims, because I love science and critical thinking. I remember a lady saying, "God healed me from cancer *twice*." I was happy for her but wanted to ask, "Really? Did he not do it right the first time? Could that have been remission? What does your doctor say?" I don't want blind faith and irrational belief.

I do believe in a God who sometimes intervenes in the natural course of events, even overruling the laws of nature which he made. The Bible has miracles on almost every page, but then it's the edited highlights from thousands of years. I don't see miracles every day. Maybe God is a bit economical with them because he respects human freedom and doesn't want to keep jumping in and over-riding our choices and their consequences. Most of God's gifts arrive quietly through natural systems the Creator originally set up. So I thank God for food, even though manna doesn't fall from the sky for me.

I think my dream was more than natural events—I'd say super-natural. Call it a minor suburban miracle if you like. It didn't stop children starving in Africa, but surely a miracle doesn't have to fix everything.

Why did God choose to intervene for us? I don't know.

What if God had not chosen to do a miracle that day? Would I still trust? I hope so—I've prayed for plenty of other things before and since that haven't come true.

29

I can't always explain why God acts as he does (or doesn't) and I wouldn't expect my little human IQ would understand. But this experience showed me beyond reasonable doubt that there is a God who sees the future and loves my son. Whatever may happen in future, nothing can take that from me.

"The secret things belong to Yahweh our God

But the things which are revealed belong to us and to our children forever."

-Moses (Deut 29:29)

8

Spit on Your Head

THE OXFORD BOAT WAS sure to lose.

Its crew wasn't organized—just a motley collection of Brit-ishers pulled together by two students who were travelling in Germany.

Richard Hillary and Frank Waldron knew a war was coming and wanted to see Europe while they could. They wrote to Herr Hitler's government asking if they could compete in a rowing race. Since the Berlin Olympics two years before had made the Nazis look good to the watching world, they were only too happy to in-vite the Oxford men. They even paid travel expenses.

Hillary and Waldron wrote to whatever rowing friends they could think of, telling them to hurry over. They arrived in the beautiful spa town of Bad Ems in dribs and drabs just two days before the event. They had done no training in weeks, and would be up against Olympic crews in what is arguably the most physi-cally demanding of all sports, the two thousand-meter men's row-ing race.

This was Germany's oldest and most prestigious rowing re-gatta, started by the king himself and called The Kaiser's Cup since 1875, but it had just been renamed the Hermann Goering Cup after the second-top Nazi. The great man himself would be there to present the shiny new cup, which had been made from an artillery shell case, gold-plated and adorned with a German eagle holding a swastika.

Busloads of supporters were arriving. Most people looked at the Britishers with contempt, but there was one friendly face who welcomed them. The local rowing coach, whose pipe and huge forearms reminded them of Popeye, was a great sport. He even spoke English.

There was one small problem. The Oxford boys hadn't managed to bring a boat. When Popeye heard this, he said, "What? You have no shell? All right, gentlemen. You leave it to me."

True to his word, he found them a racing shell. It was an older design. When they took it out for practice, they found it sat low in the water and leaked a bit, but they thanked Popeye for doing his best.

The German crews looked serious and disciplined in their brand-new boats and designer uniforms emblazoned with the swastika.

In the changing sheds before the race, one of the German rowers walked over to the Oxford crew. "Gentlemen," he said, "I have been watching you, and you are spoiled boys, lackadaisical, effete, and weakened by luxury. You are typical of the so-called upper class of your declining empire, and prime specimens of an inferior race. If we were competing in your country, we would have trained and we would win. Losing this race may not matter to you, but you can rest assured the German people are watching and will learn much from your defeat."

Hillary smiled and patted him on the shoulder. "Thanks, old chap. Though it might be wiser to boast when taking off armor than when putting it on."

But the Nazi wasn't listening.

Popeye said, "I sink you vill vin!"—and nearly drowned in the laughter of his countrymen.

The Oxford team lined up against five German boats. There was silence.

The starter's pistol fired and the hushed crowd heard the heavy wooden thud as strong young bodies uncoiled, seats rolled forward, tons of force came against rowlocks, footboards groaned, and timber hulls were shocked forward through the sparkling blue water.

The spectators found their voices. Cars and buses drove beside the river with people hanging out and shouting for Germany.

The British were so casual that they managed to fall three boat lengths behind in the first quarter of the race.

At the halfway mark the Oxford men passed under a bridge where spectators were singing "*Deutschland, Deutschland über alles.*"

The British were stone-cold last, a humiliating five boat lengths off the pace. As they passed out under the other side of the bridge, crowds jeered and laughed, and someone spat.

P-thfff!

A great glistening globule of saliva, phlegm, mucous, catarrh, cigar ash and bratwurst burst from the lips of a fat old man with Nazi insignia on his coat.

Everyone saw the shining gobbet fly through the air and land splat on the back of neck of the British cox. The crowd erupted with laughter.

The effect was exactly the opposite of what they expected. Hillary said later, "It was a tactical error."

The British showed no expression but began rowing as if every devil of hell were after them. Over the next thousand meters, they clawed back into the race, overtaking one boat after another, and crossed the finish line two-fifths of a second in front.

The crowd fell silent again.

The award ceremony was not well attended. Goering had to hand his precious cup to members of a lower race, and they had the pleasure of seeing the look on his face.

The Goering Cup sat in the trophy room of Trinity College for a year until they sent it back to the German Embassy. They wished they could fire it out of a gun because months later Hitler invaded Poland and they were at war.

Anyone doubting the courage or determination of the 1938 Trinity College boat crew need only look at their war record:

Bow: D.I. Graham, RAF pilot, killed October 1941

2: A.O.L. Stevens, RAF pilot, killed November 1940

3: R.C. Furlong, Royal Artillery, killed, Netherlands, March 1945

4: J.S. Stockton, Scots Guards, killed, North Africa, April 1943

5: H.M. 'Dinghy' Young, RAF, killed in the Dam Busters raid, May 1943

6: F.A.L. Waldron, Scots Guards, twice wounded

7: M.W. Rowe, Scots Guards

Stroke: R.H. Hillary, RAF pilot, killed January 1943

Cox: P.N. Drew-Wilkinson, RAF

This story is told in *The Last Enemy*, a book Hillary wrote in eight weeks in New York City as he worked to drum up American support for the war on Nazism. His face and hands had been badly burned in a Spitfire crash and plastic surgery was fairly basic in those days, so he could not be photographed for fear of scaring American audiences off the war. But he told great stories in radio and newspaper interviews. He also dated the actress Merle Oberon, who had been through plastic surgery herself after a car accident.

Some say he hammed up this rowing story. Either way, my mother found truth in it. If discouragement or criticism ever came our way, she would always say, "Someone spat on your head? Row harder."

The Bible says similar:

"Do not gloat over me, enemies.

Though I have fallen, I will rise.

Though I sit in darkness, the Lord will be my light" (Mic 7:8).

9

Monkey See

"DANGER! DO NOT FEED Baboons!" said the sign at the bushland area outside Cape Town, South Africa.

Baboons have stronger jaws than lions, so I had been filming from inside the van. Yet I really needed some close-ups. The troop all looked pretty calm today. One had climbed onto my bonnet and fallen asleep above the warm engine.

So I stepped out and set up my camera.

The Alpha male swaggered over and glared at me. I had been told not to look a baboon in the eye because they find that threatening. I bent over and coughed, trying to look like I was sick and weak. The Alpha ignored me, and so did the rest of his troop.

I filmed their romances, their fights, their quest for more food and better homes. It was like any reality TV show—just hairier.

When I stopped to reload my camera, I was shocked to see about fifty Japanese tourists standing right behind me, cameras at the ready. They had seen me in the wild and decided it would be safe to follow.

One guy pushed right in front of me and blocked the camera. I called out "Excuse me. . .," but he had all the confidence. I'd met another Alpha.

He reached out his hand to pat a baby baboon. It jumped away in shock, and I knew trouble was on its way. Mum appeared, shorter than Schwarzenegger but with stronger arms. She screamed in warning. The man tried again to pat her baby, looking her right in the eye to say he could be trusted. She bared her gigantic teeth and gave a shriek that chilled my blood. He smiled his most charming smile and tried again. She took an open-handed swing which landed with a loud *thwop*. He squealed and leapt back holding his thigh.

I couldn't believe his next move. He tried to pat the mother. Maybe he hoped to show he was a kind friend and this was all a misunderstanding, but she wasn't having it. He was lucky she didn't start throwing heavyweight hooks at his head, but this mother thought he only needed a spanking. She started smashing open-handed blows onto his legs and backside. Each palm strike had enough force to knock him forward half a step, which actually helped him by speeding up his sprint to the bus. Her mighty right clobbered him one final time and knocked him flying up the stairs, and the bus driver closed the door with a relieved hiss. As the bus pulled away, fifty nervous faces watched out the windows, one of them still looking surprised at the rejection.

Mum trotted back to her family cackling.

I only wish I'd filmed it.

Soon another bus arrived. They had seen the first bus leaving but hadn't seen the near-disaster, so they all rushed out excitedly. I worried for their safety, and felt a bit responsible for starting the trend they were now copying. They were Europeans, so I tried saying no in every language I knew: Nein! Non! Nyet! Ne! But they ignored me and I watched the same story happen again. The friendliest person was slapped and the rest left in panic.

It happened to another bus, then another, but they kept following each other. Tourist see, tourist do.

I left the area, hoping that all the primates—baboons and tourists—would settle down.

When I came back an hour later, buses and camper vans were still coming, not knowing what had happened to those who'd gone before.

I saw a man jump out of his camper van and start taking happy snaps. He left one window open a crack, and a small simian hand reached through it and unlocked the door. Two adult baboons got into his camper, opened his bar fridge, sat on his comfy chairs, and started scoffing his food. Please believe me when I tell you they even opened his ring-pull beers and swigged their frothy contents, chattering excitedly. After that I almost expected them to pick up a remote and watch the football.

The driver saw all this and looked shocked. He shouted "Shoo!" waving his hands. I shouted in warning, but he ignored me. It was his camper and he had rights. The baboon had a right too—a straight right Mike Tyson would envy. It thudded off the man's rib cage and bounced him out onto the ground on his backside. A scream, huge bared fangs, baboon swinging punches, tourist running. It was a total mess.

But vehicles kept coming. Human see, human do.

That happens a lot. You can copy movie star morals without checking whether they really make those people happy long-term. You can drive like that boy racer does today without seeing his funeral notice tomorrow. You can look over the fence and buy what they bought without considering whether you can afford it, and drown in debt.

The Bible says, "Do not let the world squeeze you into its mold, but be transformed by renewing your mind" (Rom 12:2).

God gave us humans the ability to think for ourselves, to work out what is right, and to choose—our major advantage over baboons. (Other than looks—in most cases.)

10

Gelert

PRINCE LLEWELLYN BLEW A long blast on his hunting horn. *Boooooooooooooop!*

Any second now his giant grey wolfhound would come bounding out of the house, skid to a stop beside him, and sit there looking impatient, his enormous body twitching with enthusiasm and energy he could barely contain. His name was Gelert, and the prince would scratch him behind the ears as friends and servants arrived with other dogs.

Gelert was an Irish wolfhound. He was so valuable that King John of England had presented him to Prince Llewellyn of Wales as a wedding gift when he married his daughter Joan in AD1210.

But where was he?

When the prince gave the signal, the men and the coursing pack of greyhounds and bulldogs, mastiffs and lurchers would head off into the forest. Gelert would lope along beside his master's horse, watching for the slightest expression or hand gesture which he would enthusiastically obey.

If a deer showed, Gelert would be off as soon as Llewellyn pointed one finger. He had the speed to keep up with a buck as it dodged and darted through the forest, and the stamina to follow it for miles across the roughest country. When the deer slowed, Gelert would move in closer. The deer would swing its antlers to hammer him in the face or spear him in his flanks. Many good dogs had been killed in this way, but Gelert knew how to duck and dodge until the deer was off balance, then lunge for its throat. His enormous jaws would lock around its windpipe and his teeth would puncture its carotid artery, quickly ending its life. Sometimes other dogs would arrive in time to help him, and the deer would have to fight on two or three sides, but usually they would hear Gelert baying in triumph and would run toward the sound. Dogs and men would come puffing into a clearing only to find the deer on the ground and Gelert standing over it.

They would carry the deer home, roast it for the prince's family, and give portions to the men for theirs. Gelert would go back to his usual role as Llewellyn's most faithful friend and the guardian of his home. Princess Joan loved Gelert, and hand-fed him from their table. Their little son Daffydd was just learning to walk and Gelert would stand beside him to support his wobbly footsteps, and would not flinch when the boy grabbed handfuls of his fur for support. Daffydd would sit with the enormous hound curled around him and scratch his ears like he saw his father do. When he tried poking curious fingers into the dog's nose and eyes, Gelert had pulled his head away but shown no sign of anger. Daffydd would put his face close to a mouth big enough to swallow him whole, and would laugh as Gelert licked him. At night Gelert slept within a few footsteps of the family, always alert in case a wolf, a thief or an enemy tried their luck.

But where was Gelert now? Llewellyn felt irritated and blew another blast on the horn. *Boooooooooooop!*

Still Gelert was nowhere to be found, and the pack had arrived. Men stood around talking as dogs yelped and yowled. Llewellyn's temper flared. What could have gotten into the pea-brained mutt? Well, there was no more time to wait. He gave the signal to be off, and the pack moved forward without their best hunter.

It was no surprise that the hunt went badly. They saw a large stag but the dogs were unable to bring it down. Worse still, two of the dog pack had their guts ripped out by antlers and had to be put out of their misery. This put everyone in a foul mood. For all their effort, they had just two rabbits in the bag. Llewellyn decided they might as well hie off home.

When he returned, no one greeted him at his door. He walked in to find no one downstairs. What on earth was going on?

He strode angrily up the stairs, only to see Princess Joan leaning against the wall, sobbing her heart out. When her husband said her name and gently touched her, she jumped in fright, saw it was him, and wordlessly pointed to their baby's bedroom.

Rushing in, Llewellyn saw absolute chaos. The baby's wooden crib was knocked over against the wall. Fresh blood soaked the bedclothes, pooled on the floor, and was splattered around the walls. Curtains had been ripped down and were twisted into the mess on the floor.

Little Daffydd was nowhere to be seen.

In terror and rage, Llewellyn paced the entire room and rummaged around in the bedclothes. He could not find his little boy.

In the corner of his eye he saw movement, and turned to see Gelert slowly standing up in a corner. The enormous dog's eyes were wild and his jaws and face were bright red with blood. Fresh gore stained the fur all across his throat and chest. He tried to smile at Llewellyn, revealing blood on his teeth.

Only one thought made sense. Gelert must have gone wild and eaten the baby boy. He was trying to wag his tail at his master, and looking pleased with himself.

"How could you!" yelled Llewellyn, drawing his sword and thrusting it into Gelert's side.

Gelert looked at him with eyes full of love and pain, and his dying howl echoed around the prince's house and cut everyone right to the heart.

As Gelert lay dying, Llewellyn heard another sound and knew he was going insane. It sounded like the snuffly little grunts his son made when he was waking up. But he must be imagining that in his grief.

Then he thought he heard his little boy cry out. But no, that was impossible. Following the sound, he lifted the heavy oak crib and saw his little son smiling sleepily at him and stretching out his arms to be picked up. The prince snatched him up and checked that he was unharmed, saying not a word as the baby chattered and burbled to him. He held him to his heart, then walked out and placed him in the arms of his mother. Her face showed shock and delight.

Looking around the baby's room once more, Llewellyn noticed in one corner a black wolf. It was even bigger than Gelert. Its teeth were still bared in attack, and it looked wildly threatening even though its eyes were glassy and its throat had recently been torn out.

☙ ❧

Wouldn't it be sad to misunderstand your savior?

But many people did that with Jesus from the start, calling him Mary's illegitimate son, uneducated, a fake miracle worker fooling people, demon-possessed, insane, a threat to Roman peace or a mere man claiming to be God. He was criticized or ignored, and leaders eventually nailed him, executing him the most painful way they could.

Yet just days later, friends claimed they had seen him alive again. Their fear and cowardice at his death turned to a boldness that would take them all over the world telling the story of his resurrection, even when they were threatened with death. They were sure enough to stand up in the same city where he had been killed—where anyone could fact-check their claims—and they told a crowd of people, "You need to know the fact that God has made this Jesus—the one you crucified—both Lord and Messiah."

Oops! You killed him, God resurrected him. It seems you religious leaders are working against God.

When the people heard this, they were cut to the heart, and they asked Peter and the other apostles what they should do.

Peter said, "Say sorry and get baptized, each of you, in the name of Jesus Christ for the forgiveness of your sins, and you will receive the gift of the Holy Spirit. This promise is for you and your children, and anyone who is far away. . ." (Acts 2:36–39).

It's for us today too.

11

Oink

I WASN'T REALLY PAYING attention as we waited to cross Pennant Hills Road. I was joking around with my schoolmate Geoff.

A vile stench hit us. We groaned and turned our heads to see what it was.

An old farm truck was pulling up at the lights with its brakes whining. At that exact moment some of the boards in its sidewall creaked and gave way, and eleven fat pigs poured out like a river of bacon, flowing onto the bonnet of the Volvo station wagon in the next lane.

Ten of them bounced, rolled off onto their trotters, and trotted off through the traffic, grunting and oinking. One lay still on the dented bonnet with its neck twisted and dead eyes staring at the lady driving the Volvo. Her children grimaced and pointed.

A farmer jumped out of the truck and said to her, "Pleasa, you wait, lady. Ima comin' back."

He looked at his pigs, which had shot past us with surprising speed and were escaping into the quiet, leafy suburb of Beecroft. He called out, "Hey, yousa boys. You catcha my pigs, I giva you hundred bucks eacha one."

That seemed like a lot of money, so we went pig-hunting in Beecroft.

We found the first porky escapee on someone's lawn. It charged at us, clearly enjoying its freedom too much to go back. This was just like football, but the player weighed 140 kg and had twice as many legs. I said, "You take legs, I'll take body and—OOOOF!"

I got my arms around its greasy neck. It was slippery but I held on, accidentally getting a look up its nostril. Hamboogers. I still need counseling about that.

Geoff grabbed one leg but the other three kept running, and one trod on his hand. "Ow! Pig on someone your own size!" he said, grabbing both front legs with new determination. The pig somersaulted. So did Geoff and I, but we didn't let go of $100.

Geoff said, "Aw, that hit me so hard I've got hamnesia."

The farmer ran over and hog-tied it. "Gooda boys! Keepa goin', uh?"

The second one was easy. We chased it into Atkinson's place and it didn't see their swimming pool. It swam around for a while until we led it up the pool steps and the farmer roped it.

A third pig tried to run through Mrs Rabinowicz's hedge and got its head stuck. She shouted in Polish-English, encouraging us not the pig—she was Jewish. It tried to kick us but we tied its back legs and held it until the farmer arrived.

I lassoed the fourth one. It ran right past me and I simply slipped a loop over its neck, accidentally discovering the sport of lawn ski-ing. The pig tired of it before I did.

Our fifth porker ran down a driveway into someone's carport. We thought we had it cornered, but it shoved its huge backside through the wall and reversed out to freedom. Geoff and I were waiting. "Hambush," said Geoff. As we dropped it to the ground, he said, "Careful. Don't go bacon its heart."

Geoff saw our sixth pig digging up Mr Toft's prize roses. He threw himself into the tackle at great personal sacrifice. "Don't worry about the scratches," I said, "your mum will put on some oinkment." It was his turn to groan.

In the end we found all but one. Perhaps it was eaten by the predators of Beecroft—manipulative physiotherapists, criminal lawyers or the Hell's Accountants motorcycle gang. I don't suspect Mrs. Rabinowicz.

We went home with a lot of money for our piggy banks. The farmer must have paid out thousands more for damages—more than it would have cost to build strong walls on his truck.

Words can be like pigs, escaping and causing damage. Angry words can make a fight much worse, rip up a working relationship, or shred someone's confidence and self-respect for a long time. Telling secrets to untrustworthy people can really cost you. Gossip and lies can damage a reputation, a relationship or a career. Speech is so serious that it's mentioned in two of the Ten Commandments.

Once words have escaped, you can't catch them, even though sometimes you'd be willing to pay $100 a word. You might be able to apologize, but often you can't always repair the damage. I can understand why the Bible often praises careful, kind, thoughtful speech, and why one Bible character prays

"God, put a guard over my mouth.

Build a strong gate around my lips" (Ps 141:3).

12

Bear

A LONG-HAIRED GERMAN SHEPHERD named Bear was at home when he heard weird noises coming from the roof.

A stranger had climbed up there, removed some tiles and slid inside.

Bear kept quiet. He watched as legs poked through a manhole in the ceiling, and a man dropped through and started eyeing the entertainment cabinet. Bear quietly padded up behind him and growled like a bulldozer starting its engine.

The burglar's adrenaline fired and he jumped so high that he found himself scrabbling onto the top of the cabinet, swearing feebly and shaking in fear, but grateful he still had his throat.

Nice, but now what? He couldn't reach the manhole. He couldn't walk away. He couldn't even relax for a second because the giant woofer might jump onto the cabinet at any time and he had to be ready to fend it off with a boot or a fist. Maybe if he found a good enough weapon—but there was nothing like that. He would just have to wait there until it got hungry and went away.

But Bear knew better. His master, Dave, was a dog trainer at a security company, and Bear had been top of his class. He was devastating in attack, yet so gentle and intelligent and fun-loving that Dave had brought him home to guard his family.

Bear sat and watched patiently.

The burglar was sure the owners would be back soon and call off the big chomper, and then he could bolt. He looked at his watch (or probably someone else's). It was 2pm Friday.

On Monday afternoon, Dave's family drove in from their long weekend at the beach.

The next-door neighbor came over to the car, concerned. "Is Bear OK? We haven't seen him all weekend. . ."

Dave strode inside to see. Bear looked fine, but did not take his eyes off whatever he was guarding. Dave followed Bear's gaze and was surprised to see a man sitting on top of the entertainment cabinet. He hadn't eaten or drunk anything at all for three days. He hadn't made it to the bathroom. He hadn't slept either, and tears were rolling down his face. He whispered through his dry throat, "Help me."

He could wait another minute.

"Good boy, Bear," said Dave. "Release."

Bear instantly dashed out the back doggie door towards the lemon tree. His self-control had been much better than the burglar's.

Bear drained his water bowl. He chomped some dried food. And within a couple of minutes he headed straight back inside to report for duty.

The burglar was climbing down until he saw Bear come back. He groaned and climbed back up onto the cabinet, sniveling that it wasn't fair.

When the police arrived, they found a burglar refusing to get down from a cupboard until they could keep him safe.

They kept him inside for a couple of years. Imagine him getting panic attacks every time Lassie or Scoobie Doo came on the prison TV.

Like Bear, believers are waiting for their Master to return. And waiting. And waiting. Some people say, "The Master is really taking his time." Some give up their belief, and start acting like this life is all they will ever have.

But Jesus said, "I will return. Keep busy till I come." And the Bible says, "We must not become weary doing good. We will receive eternal life eventually if we don't give up" (Matt 24:45–51; John 14:1–3; Luke 19:13; Gal 6:9).

13

Victoria's Secret

VICTORIA WAS FOUR FEET eleven inches of Greek goddess, and five inches of that was hair.

She was about sixty years old and wore the banana-yellow uniform of the public hospital cleaner. I met her when I was driving food trucks and washing up all day in the summer before university started.

For eight hours a day minus breaks, Victoria worked with an orbital floor polisher, a hunk of metal twice the size of my lawn-mower. It had two wheels to transport it when it wasn't working, but when it was switched on, it helicoptered along on a spinning pad, shining the floors.

Victoria piloted her heavy weapon with three nonchalant fingers, the other hand in her pocket, a cigarette in the corner of her mouth. She could put it where she wanted it just by thinking about it, and I said, "Wow, you make it look easy."

It was a mistake.

"Easy! Easy, you think, huh?" she said, her smile replaced by a sneer. "Well, you try it then, Mr Smarty Skippy Boy."

"No no, Victoria, I was trying to say that I bet it's hard but your skill makes it *look* easy. It was a compliment."

"Sure," she grunted, as she shoved the control handles my way.

Well, OK then, how hard can it. . . *Vreeeeeeeeem!* She had switched it on before I knew it, and the stupid contraption spun me round and round like a puppet. I was bush-dancing with Godzilla.

Loops of power cord were wrapping around me like an octopus on his honeymoon, but I managed to hit the off switch and everything slowed down. I was able to unwrap myself.

Victoria laughed so hard she had to lean on a wall.

"Next dance?" she finally asked, barely interrupting her two-pack-a-day cackle.

"Delighted," I said, bowing to her. I was eighteen years old and playing rugby—in fact I was a forward in the front row of the scrum and thought I was pretty tough. If little old Victoria could hold this dumb machine, surely I could! I widened my stance, braced my shoulders, held on tight. . .

Vreeeeeeeeeeeeeeeeeem!

And I held it!

When I lifted one foot to take a step, the force almost spun me around, so I quickly put the foot back down. I inched down the hall using baby steps. It was very hard work but I was winning—until the spinning pad touched the edge of a nursing trolley, which crashed over in a cacophony of falling bedpans that sounded like the end of the world. The polisher careened around in crazed circles. I couldn't hold it, and had to jump into the air to avoid it taking out my shins. I believe I may have screamed out in panic before it slammed into a wall.

Victoria laughed so hard I thought she'd wheeze up a lung.

I sheepishly picked up the trolley and the bedpans. How on earth did she do it so easily? There must be a trick here that I didn't know.

When Victoria saw I was humbled, she walked over, stood up on tip-toes and imparted her wisdom.

"Don't fight it," she said. "Balance it." And she wobbled her hand from side to side.

That's it?

49

So I tried again. As the machine switched on, I fought it hard at first. Then by twisting it side to side, I found an angle where it stopped fighting me back. Aaah! Easy!

"Kala, Skippy!" beamed Victoria. "Good!"

"Thanks, Victoria," I beamed. It was almost effortless.

It was so easy that I got lazy and lost the angle for a while and the pressure hit me. But instead of fighting it, I quickly balanced it. Now I knew where that sweet spot was. Twist. Balance. Easy.

Life can be hard work. There is no shortage of opposition in the outside world, and sometimes we feel we're fighting against parts of ourselves. I can only say that I find connecting with God can rebalance me and help me operate in my sweet spot. Grunt and grit are admirable and all, but happiness is ultimately the result of God's kind care, and of loving, generous relationships with others. And afterlife can't be achieved by work and effort, but only by trusting God's forgiving kindness. I should put my effort into finding those, not fighting life.

Balance yourself. That's the secret Victoria told me.

And Jesus said, "Come to me, anyone who is stressed and overloaded, and I will give you rest. Take my yoke on you, and learn from me, because I am gentle and humble in heart, and you will find rest for your soul, since I carry my load easily and I find my heavy burden light" (Matt 11:28–29).

14

Give My Bum a Push

THIS IS NOT MY story. My namesake uncle told it to me with half a lung during his last illness, always charming and entertaining, even when gasping from an oxygen bottle and craving cigarettes.

⬸ ⬷

George Sharpe lived next door to us. He had spent three years as a machine gunner in World War I, and had shell-shock to prove it. If a car backfired, he might dive under the kitchen table screaming. It would take him a minute to get on top of his PTSD and to realize where he was.

One day he asked me how school was going.

"Alright," I fibbed.

"Who's your principal?"

"Mr Mearns," I said.

"Mearns? Not Norman Roscoe Mearns?"

"Mr N. R. Mearns. Yes, I think so."

"Well, well, well! Captain Norman Roscoe "Give-My-Bum-A-Push" Mearns.

"What?"

"My boy, he was my captain at the Battle of Pozieres. Cared for all us boys like we was his own sons. Cunning as a dunny rat. And courage! He's a little short fella, right?"

"Yeah. He has to stand on a box in his office to cane the six-footers." (I didn't say how I knew that.)

"That'd be right. In the trenches, he wanted to see what the enemy was up to, so he'd clamber up on an ammo box and try to look over the top—using a periscope, of course, coz a bullet hole in the forehead could be a bit inconvenient. But the ammo box would sway around in the mud, and Mearns would see some big tall farmboy standing around in uniform and he'd yell out, 'I say, Private, give my bum a push! Give my bum a push!' The soldier would have to hold him up by the fundament for as long as he needed."

Mr Mearns had never mentioned his war service, even on Anzac Day, so I kept quiet about it too. But a week later a friend and I got into trouble. Again.

My friend was shorter, so Mr Mearns picked up the cane and gave him six of the best. "Out!" he bellowed. "Behave yourself."

"Yes, sir."

He turned to me. "Well?" he boomed. "Get the box."

I put it near his desk but I didn't put my hand out for a caning.

"Well, Kent, what are you waiting for?"

I had nothing to lose, so I took a gamble. "Well, sir, if you're going to stand on the box, I was wondering if I should give your bum a push."

He slumped, dropped the cane and looked at me in shock. "Where did you hear that?"

I told him I knew George Sharpe.

Mr Mearns sat on the desk and talked to me, telling me stories about the war, about fear and courage, about losing comrades, about discipline, obedience and respect. He talked to me man-to-man for an hour. He didn't even cane me.

I looked up to little Mr Mearns after that, and behaved myself impeccably in his school. I had so much respect for him now that I didn't want to disappoint him.

❧   ❧

Sixty years later, watching my Uncle Gren smile into his oxygen mask at the memory of Mr Mearns, it hit me that I used to think of

God as a grumpy old school principal caning everyone for breaking his silly rules, until I understood he had suffered and sacrificed and died for others like the soldiers we remember. Jesus died slowly on a cross to pay for our mistakes and to give us eternal life. When you see who he really is, you respect and love him and want to show that by living well.

"If you love me," Jesus said, "keep my commandments" (John 14:15).

15

Mike Adalna's Shoes

SOMEONE WAS KNOCKING ON the front door of Judge Samuel Liebowitz's Long Island mansion.

He wasn't expecting anyone. It was a snowy December night, and he was relaxing with his wife and three children.

He opened the small inspection portal. Through the safety bars he saw a skinny, whiskered face shivering in the cold.

"Remember me, Your Honor?"

"Mike Adalna," said Liebowitz. "Has it been seven years already?"

❧   ❧

Seven years earlier, before he was made a judge, Liebowitz had been a defense attorney. Adalna was facing the death penalty for murder and robbery, and Liebowitz agreed to defend him.

The facts were that Adalna broke into a store to steal some food. The owner came downstairs and tried to stop him, and Adalna hit him with a bag full of cans and ran away. The owner was an old man and he hit his head on the floor and died. Police caught Adalna nearby, eating food from a can.

In court, Liebowitz explained that Adalna was desperate because he was unemployed and had not eaten for over a week. He had not meant to harm the old man and felt deep remorse that he had caused his death. He was not a criminal, and this was his first offense.

Instead of being hanged for murder, Adalna was convicted of manslaughter and sentenced to seven years hard labor.

He did his time, and now he was standing at Liebowitz's door.

"Judge, I got out ten days ago and I've come to see you because I'm desperate. I haven't eaten for six days. If I can't get food, my choices will be to starve or to steal it, and this time I might not be so lucky. I'm willing to work hard, but no one wants to hire an ex-con. What does a fella have to do if he wants to start again?"

Liebowitz rubbed his chin. "They must have taught you a trade in prison."

"Yes, broom-making. There are two broom factories in New York and I've been to both of 'em but they're not hiring. I've gone from door to door every day looking for work, offering to do anything at all, but no one's hiring. I'm not asking for charity. I just need a break."

"Hmmm," said Liebowitz, not looking convinced.

Mike held one foot up high so the judge could see it. His shoe had a top but no sole, and his foot was red raw from days of walking on icy pavements. That couldn't be faked. His other foot was the same.

"I'm not lying, Judge."

Liebowitz opened the door, allowing a convicted killer into his family home.

He led Adalna into the warm kitchen, heated the leftovers of his family's dinner and filled a large dinner plate, adding slices of bread and cheese. Adalna emptied it minutes. Liebowitz filled it again.

He showed Adalna into a glistening white bathroom and filled the tub. When he left, Adalna slid through the layer of bubbles into his first hot bath for more than seven years.

The bathroom door opened a crack and Liebowitz placed a shaving kit on the bench, hung a suit of clothes on a peg and slid a pair of shoes onto the floor. "Try these. We're about the same size."

When Adalna could drag himself out of the bath, he shaved off his stubble, barely recognizing the face that smiled back. He put on a lawyer's suit with a Saks Fifth Avenue label. He laced up soft leather shoes. With soles.

Liebowitz was in his study calling a friend who owned a gas station. The friend said, "I'm not hiring, Sam, but as a favor to you, no problem. Send him round at 8am tomorrow."

At 7am next morning, Adalna reported for work. He worked fast and was friendly and helpful to the customers. When they saw his suit, they were flattered to be served by the owner.

He gave great service every working day for the next two years, though he swapped the suit for a uniform. Not a penny ever went missing.

The owner gave him raise after raise and made him manager of that gas station. A few years after that, the owner gave him a loan and helped him start his own business.

Adalna found love, married and had children. When he retired, he owned six gas stations and employed dozens of people. None of them knew about his past. They knew him as a fair, generous boss with one funny quirk. Every Christmas he always gave his employees the same gift—a quality pair of shoes. He sent a pair to Judge Liebowitz as well, just in case someone else was knocking on his door.

The world needs a judge to get rid of injustice, but we need one who can deal with our mistakes and encourage us.

The bad news is we are all guilty of sin, and the Bible says the penalty for sin is death. The unbelievably good news is that Jesus took that death penalty instead of each of us, so we could live forever. So the judge can declare us not guilty and not punish us, while still being just. Because Christ died for us, God can "remain just and yet also justify people who trust Jesus" (Rom 3:26).

That's how "mercy triumphs over judgment" (Jas 2:12–13).

16

The High Flier

HE HAD BEEN HAMMERING away with all his strength for hours.

Eventually he heard a crack and felt the wall give way. He pushed his face through the hole he had made, and got a glimpse of his mother. She looked so nice and sang to him so sweetly that he was encouraged to keep pushing and, within minutes, he was lying on the floor of their home, totally exhausted. He looked at his mother with immense love and happiness. He couldn't wait to spend time with her and his father, and his many brothers and sisters.

He had really come out of his shell recently.

When his mother finished dropping a worm into the open mouth of one of his brothers, she came over and looked at him. She immediately started pushing him along the floor towards the edge of their home.

Hi, Mum! Mum? Is something wrong?

She shoved him out of the house and he started falling towards the ground far below.

Nooooooo! Muuuuuum!

He panicked and got into a real flap, but nothing slowed his fall.

Thud! He hit the ground. The impact nearly killed him, and he lay there trying to gather the strength to move.

An ant arrived and started biting into his flesh. Other ants came, climbing all over his body and eating him. This was serious.

He wasn't going to die today—no way. He would have to think of something...

⟡   ⟡

A human mum saw a baby bird lying on the footpath. He had no feathers, and ants were swarming all over him, even into his beak and throat. He was wiggling, trying to get rid of the attacking ants, and she thought he had a determined look in his eye. She picked him up and flicked the ants off.

"Poor little fella," she said. Looking closer, she noticed that his determined eye was the only one he had.

Curious, she looked up. High above in a tree was a nest, and a mother bird was feeding her chicks. She must have decided not to waste food on this damaged one-eyed chick, thinking he wouldn't survive anyway.

The human mum decided to take him home to her nest with her young. She gave him water, then bread with honey, then mashed egg. He ate with gusto, even biting the spoon.

The human mum's children named him Tim. They hoped he might be a parrot with a designer wardrobe of flashy colors, but he grew the brown and grey feathers of an ordinary sparrow.

Tim seemed to think he was human, probably because humans were his only family and he had no bird example to follow. But this meant he only ever walked.

"How can we teach him to fly?" the children asked. "We don't know that ourselves."

When Tim had all his feathers, their dad tried an idea. He stood up on a stool and dropped the little bird out of his hand. Tim must have thought, *Nooo, I'm being thrown away again!* But even in his panic, he tried his best. He flapped his little wings as hard as he could. Before he hit the floor, one of the children caught him.

They repeated this and it became a game. Tim still tried his hardest and didn't seem worried. Soon he was able to slow his fall a bit. As he grew stronger muscles, he was able to stop avoid hitting the ground at all. He started making short flights on his own, then longer and longer leaps until he could fly.

"I wish I could do that," said the children.

Tim became a stunt pilot. He could land gently on moving heads, which looked as skillful as landing a fighter jet on an aircraft carrier. He could even land on bald heads, though the runway had less traction and there were dramatic shouts and screams the first few times until he learned not to use his claws.

Tim became family. He flew into the parents' bedroom at 6am each morning and start tugging at the mum's hair, singing, *Let's go! Get up! It's going to be a great day!*

When guests came for dinner, Tim greeted each one by turns, landing on their heads and singing a song. People said that they could not believe that an ordinary old sparrow with one eye had such personality.

When the family went out for a walk, Tim flew from tree to tree above them, then turned for home when they did. He landed on a head just before they walked in their front door.

One sad day, the dad was reading in the garden and Tim was sitting on his finger. A neighbor's cat saw his chance. He snuck up on Tim's blind side, getting closer and closer, and launched. His claws slashed across Tim's belly, opening a huge gash before ending up in the dad's finger.

The dad yelled in pain and gave the cat a flying lesson.

Tim's intestines were hanging out in loops on the ground but he had his tough face on. *We'll get through this.*

The dad rushed next door to where a retired nurse lived. He had only a basic first aid kit, but he found a needle and thread in a sewing kit and cleaned Tim up with methylated spirits. As the dad held Tim's innards in, the nurse carefully sewed.

Tim survived his operation without any anesthetic, and was flying again within fifteen minutes.

One happy day the family went for a walk/fly and Tim saw his first female sparrow. The children thought he looked as shocked as if he had flown smack into a glass window.

Down below, the family worried she might reject him for his missing eye, but Tim was as confident as ever, flying right up to her and singing with great brio, "I only have eye for you."

She must have liked his song. After a brief victory lap, they flew off together.

The family missed him, and worried whether he had the skills to survive in the wild.

But most days they glimpsed him rushing around finding food for the love of his life and their half-dozen perfect young in the great nest he had made.

"You can buy two sparrows for a dollar, but I'm telling you that when one of them falls to the ground, your father in heaven notices. So you can be confident, because you are worth even more to Him than sparrows."

-Jesus (Luke 12:6–7)

17

Letting Go

MY FRIEND MARK ("THE Shark") adores seafood. He drools at the sight of weird critters swimming behind glass at Chinese restaurants, and knows all their names—bony fish and non-bony fish, crustaceans like lobsters and crayfish, mollusks like clams, oysters, mussels, snails, and cephalopods like octopus and squid.

He learned scuba diving and spearfishing so he could catch his own, becoming a top predator of the sea.

One weekend he was diving off a Sydney beach and saw a crab that was bigger than a family pizza. (I doubted this until I checked: "Can grow to 5.5 kilograms.")

He quickly grabbed it by its back, avoiding pincers powerful enough to break his fingers. All it could do was wave its claws around uselessly and tickle his hand with its back legs and swimmerlets.

Mark was keen to take home his prize, so he started up towards the surface. He knew he had to come up bit by bit to avoid decompression sickness or "the bends." He was down quite deep, and the water was putting a lot of pressure on his body. If he came up too fast and the pressure on him dropped too quickly, the gases in his blood could expand and bubble up. It would be like opening a bottle of lemonade, which drops the pressure in the bottle and makes bubbles come out of the drink—only the bubbles would be coming out of his blood and could damage many parts of his body. This could be fatal, so Mark took his time.

Just then another huge crab appeared. Mark couldn't believe his luck. He turned, caught it with his free hand and grinned behind his mask. *Entrée and main course!*

At about twenty-five meters depth, he was resting and wondering what crab recipes to use when he found to his horror that he couldn't breathe. Had his tank run out of air? He looked down and saw a huge pincer was clamped across his air hose. He must have let the first crab get too close when he was chasing the second.

He sucked with all his strength, going red in the face, but the seal was airtight. He had only seconds to act.

He tried to pull the crab off, but its grip on the hose was better than his grip on its slippery back.

What to do? If he fought too much, he could lose both crabs. No way!

So Mark took a massive risk. He blasted upwards to the surface, swam to his dinghy, clubbed both crabs to death on the side of the boat, threw them in, and then desperately dived down again to get more water pressure on his body and hopefully beat decompression sickness.

He felt his lungs burning and prickling as if someone was stabbing them with a million pins. His skin went hot and cold. His joints ached and his muscles wouldn't do what he wanted. Worst of all, he started to feel light-headed. He fought to keep his brain from going foggy, knowing that if you faint while diving alone, you probably never wake up. But somehow he managed to stay conscious and calm. He stayed down at that level, hoping to equalize the gas pressures in his body.

When he surfaced, he felt so rubbish that he took himself to hospital. They rushed him into a hyperbaric chamber, basically a sealed room where they increase the air pressure and let you breathe pure oxygen.

The doctor said Mark was very lucky not to injure his inner ear, which could have damaged his hearing and his balance for the rest of his life.

But as Mark lay in hospital, what really hurt was the memory of surfacing, climbing over the side of his dingy, and seeing three large seagulls flap away, struggling to take off after such a huge gourmet lunch of crab.

Are there things we should just let go? Habits that harm us or others? Addictions that keep us from maximum well-being? Greed and overwork that takes time we could spend on relationships? Laziness and self-indulgence that block good ambitions? Sins we think will make us happy, against common sense and God's advice?

"We should just let go of everything that slows us down, and the sin that so easily tangles us up, and follow Jesus. . . He put up with dying on a cross and ignored all the public shaming because he knew how much happiness that would bring in the future" (Heb 12:1–2).

18

Jambo, Jumbo

A PEARL BLUE MERCEDES-BENZ saloon drove into the Zimbabwe game park where Moses Mpofu worked. As it passed his guard post, his expert nose told him something was seriously wrong.

He walked over and found the driver picking a bug out of the radiator grille of his brand-new vehicle. "Good morning, sir," said Moses.

"You will guard my car well, yes?" The driver spoke loudly and slowly as if Moses were slow.

"Yes, sir, with your cooperation. Perhaps you noticed the sign as you drove in: 'Do not leave fruit in vehicles.' I was wondering. . ."

"What I eat or do not eat, what I have or do not have is none of your concern. Do your job."

"Perhaps I could explain. . .," Moses began.

"Listen to me. I am a foreign diplomat and I am not bound by the rules of your country." He tried to sound like the ambassador when in fact he was an embassy clerk.

"Sir, if. . ."

The driver held up his hand. "Enough. I am covered by diplomatic immunity. Now, I am late for my tour." And without any diplomacy at all he walked off towards the waiting Land Rover.

🐘 🐘

About ten kilometers away, Nyasha the elephant and her young son Chatunga were enjoying a meal of grass.

Nyasha stopped and smelled the breeze, using a nose more powerful than any other mammal's. She could smell water and food from many kilometers away, and could decide whether a source was worth the long walk. From a safe distance, she could smell the difference between tribes who traditionally hunted elephants and those who didn't. And if a tourist got too close to her son, she would remember his smell and avoid him all day, even recognizing him if he came back the next year.

What she was smelling now was driving her wild. Just a few molecules of it floating on the breeze would jangle the scent cells in her nose—she had twice as many as a bloodhound—and light up the massive olfactory bulb in her brain, promising pleasure that it was practically impossible for her to resist.

Oranges!

Chatunga could smell them too. His body was swaying with pleasure and longing.

They set off, the mother proud of her son's speed. Before long they were strolling silently into the car park on their gelatin-padded feet.

Moses had been expecting them, or one of their family. He smiled and shook his head, knowing from experience what was about to happen. "Exactly," he said to himself, never even thinking of using the rifle slung over his shoulder.

Alright, my boy, where are they?

In one of those strange metal horses that humans ride, mother.

Yes.

This blue one.

Chatunga ran his trunk along the side of the Mercedes, feeling around and gently pushing. Unlike his mother, he hadn't touched a car before. One of the windows smashed in. The car alarm sounded, and Chatunga jumped back in panic.

But nothing happened and his mother stayed calm, so he learned to ignore it. He snaked his trunk into the car's cabin and felt around, finding nothing because the oranges were in the boot.

Shall I try? Nyasha slid her trunk in and pulled on the back of the rear seat until—*Oing!*—it came away. But she could only touch the cold steel firewall of the boot, not the oranges. She pulled out and went around to the rear of the car.

If at first you don't succeed, try. . .

She lifted her head and suddenly slammed it down, spearing her tusks through the steel lid of the boot. Then she gave a mighty lift. Some Stuttgart engineer reading this will be proud to know that the boot lid stayed closed, even when the back half of a 1560kg car was lifted two meters into the air.

. . .try. . .

She shook her head around, but this boot lid stayed on.

She flung the car to the ground. It landed on its wheels. The airbags opened perfectly. This made Chatunga flinch, but his mother didn't hesitate.

. . .and try again.

Nyasha rammed her tusks in and lifted the car again, then slammed it down on its wheels, then turned her head and slammed it onto one side, then the other. She even thudded it down on its roof. She bounced it around like a toy for half an hour until at last one of its 4,900 high-strength welds broke and one corner of the boot lid opened slightly.

Half a dozen oranges rolled from the car's trunk and instantly vanished into two others.

Mother and son found that taste was definitely worth the effort, and strode happily into the jungle.

❧   ❧

A day of viewing the wonders of African wildlife had left the embassy clerk feeling at one with the universe. On a natural high, he walked back towards the car park in an awestruck reverie.

When he saw his car, he tottered around on shaky legs and could barely stand. Moses told me the man looked like he was about to faint, and went through shock, denial, rage and depression within a few minutes, then back to rage.

He couldn't blame himself or his beautiful car, but he could blame Moses. He threatened him with violence, legal action and slavery.

Moses simply said, "Sir, the sign was very clear. I tried to warn you of this repeatedly, but you would not listen. Elephants have failed to hear of your diplomatic immunity."

"Any fool is sure his plans are great, but a wise person listens to advice," says the old proverb. "Some people ruin their lives by stupidity, then blame God" (Prov 19:3; 12:15).

The best advice I've ever read comes from the Bible's book of Proverbs, a collection of inspired sayings that cover most of life and are short and witty enough to memorize and chew over through the day. See what you think.

19

All Torque

ANDREW KEPT COPPING IT in his Mechanics class.

The teacher, Mr Cusworth, didn't teach much. He was famous for saying, "If you wanna know how, read the book." Then he'd sit in his office and do crosswords.

One day Andrew said, "Sir, is there. . .?

"Have you read the book?"

"Yes, sir, but I was wondering. . ."

"Don't wonder. Read the book."

"I have, sir, but. . ."

"Then read it again."

Andrew was a top student, but a guy called Mick was a bully and a doofus and kept setting him up. He would purposely leave a mess on Andrew's desk and watch Cusworth bust and humiliate the wrong person. Finally, Andrew had had enough.

Cusworth had given each student an old lawn mower engine to repair, and one helpful hint: "If you wanna start it up, take it outside—or else."

Andrew worked hard until his engine was finely tuned. Then he removed its muffler, turned the throttle up flat out, removed the throttle lever, filled it with petrol, and set the spring-loaded starter so that it would start at the slightest bump. Then he brought it inside and wound it into the vice on his desk as if it still needed repairs.

"Mick, don't touch my motor—please," he said. Then he walked to Cusworth's office door.

"Excuse me, sir, I was wondering. . ."

"Have you read the. . ."

Click.

Brrrrrmmmmmba! RRRRUMMMMM-RRRRMMMMM!!

Cusworth jumped out of his chair, shouting. No one heard a word he said. His face reddened and veins stood out on his neck as he bellowed louder, but still he sounded like Marcel Marceau.

He charged out and found Mick fiddling with the motor, frantically groping for the throttle control. Andrew had that in his pocket, an innocent look on his face, and a better alibi than Snow White.

Other classmates fled from the room holding their ears and wanting to avoid the wrath of Cusworth. He was bearing down on Mick, who was wielding a screwdriver to try to stop the motor as it screamed in high-revving excitement.

Mick tried to pull off the spark plug lead, not knowing Andrew had soldered it on. An electric shock made him jump, squeal and drop the screwdriver.

Mick covered one ear to drop the volume of the monstrous din. He grabbed a hammer and took wild swings at the engine, but only succeeded in knocking it out of the vice. It careened across the workbench, then dropped onto the concrete floor, where it suddenly took on a life of its own.

It waltzed towards Cusworth, who jumped into the air to avoid it, but then it cannoned into a steel table and bounced back just as his feet came down, taking the bark off one of his ankles.

Mick and Cusworth chased it around the workshop, throwing brooms and other tools at it.

It was too hot to touch now, and smokier than the Red Baron's death dive.

Everyone else was outside protecting their ears and trying not to let Cusworth see them laughing.

The fuel ran out in ten minutes, but it took Cusworth longer than that to run out of angry words for Mick. He was practiced at cross words.

Some people see God as an uncaring grump in the sky, not interested in helping us, shouting angrily, "Read my book!" and punishing us even when we do our best.

Jesus was a very different kind of teacher, always encouraging people to try again because God loves them and cares about them. He said, "I didn't come here to condemn you. I came to give you life—a better life than you thought possible" (John 10:10).

20

Simply Not Good Enough!

Mr Lowe, our headmaster, was teaching mathematics to year six when a grumpy mother stormed his classroom. She had no appointment and he was obviously busy, but she stood by the door rudely drumming her heels.

We saw who it was and sighed. Mrs Alton-Nevis. (Names changed.) We knew her as a "whine and cheese" who would appear at school events, all big hair and flashing brand names, and harrumph that things were "simply not good enough"—but she never offered to help.

She could talk down to taller people. In the school concert of life, she wanted to play the princess but was tragically miscast.

Mr Lowe saw her and said, "I'll be free at recess in about fifteen minutes. . ."

"It can't wait," she piped. "It's simply not good enough, the way you've. . ."

"Excuse me, Mrs Alton-Nevis, I do have a class."

But she had none. She whined that her son had not been chosen for one of the sporting teams. She made him sound like an Olympian but we all knew he was much better at video games.

Mr Lowe calmly said, "I will be free at recess." He tried to go back to teaching us about the area of a triangle, but she interrupted him.

We all fumed. She was attacking our Mr Lowe! Right in front of us! Nobody would take that—even boys he had recently caned. Somehow Mr Lowe's canings felt like a reminder of your better self, a compliment to your potential. Don't ask me how I know that.

She ended her rant with her famous line, "It's simply not good enough." As we rolled our eyes and tried not to laugh, Mrs Alton-Nevis did a walkout, nose in the air.

It was a top-quality adult tantrum except that she tripped. Her shoe clicked loudly on something as she walked out the door. Her foot stayed stuck there while her body pitched forwards and she fought hard not to land on her face. She flung her handbag into the air. Her skirt flapped up. Her little legs bicycled frantically while her arms swam freestyle. She let out an unmodulated squawk. She went trundling heavily down the hall for quite a while until she recovered her balance.

There was a second of stupefied silence.

Then Mr Lowe pointed to the blackboard and calmly said, "The base is six meters, so half the base is three meters, see?" No one was looking or listening.

All eyes were on Mrs Alton-Nevis, who turned around, shock and embarrassment turning to fury on her face, and strode back to attack Mr Lowe some more.

But twenty-six children erupted, and our laughter proved too strong an emotional headwind. Her face fell. She picked up her handbag and fled—carefully—to the car park.

Two people were not laughing. Her son. And Mr Lowe. He held up one hand for quiet and explained that everyone has bad days and it's always better to be understanding because everyone is trying their best. The son's face showed relief.

Mr Lowe had read Jesus' words:

"Love your enemies, do good to them. . .

Then your reward will be great, and you will be true children of God, who is kind to the ungrateful and the wicked" (Luke 6:35).

At recess we looked at the doorway and found the carpet divider had a nail that was sticking up a few millimeters. We said, "That's simply not good enough," and hammered it in.

Looking back, I wonder if the real problem was that Mrs Alton-Nevis felt she was simply not good enough herself. But Mr Lowe treated everyone as worthwhile, calmly giving us wise love and steady encouragement even in our worst moments.

21

Get A Hat, Get Ahead

MY AUNT HEATHER HAD seen a hat.

Not just any old hat. It was a designer creation in the window of a boozhie boutique at the alpine ski resort of Thredbo.

She popped in and tried it on of course, and started dropping hints to her husband, my Uncle Winston. He dared to ask the price and almost choked, but an idea formed.

"If you can ski from the top of the mountain to Kareela station in three minutes, I'll buy it for you," he said.

It was an offer she couldn't refuse. She spent all week practicing, enthusiastic to tackle any slope with him. He enjoyed her company so much that the hat now seemed a bargain.

On the last day, she decided she was ready. She paused on the start line, all one hundred and fifty centimeters of her, her face as determined as an ocean-going tadpole.

"Go!" roared my uncle, looking at his watch.

Aunt Heather pushed off along the main path, then turned right and dropped straight off the lip, hurtling down the steep slope in a perfect racing crouch.

She crisply executed a dozen linked turns down the fall line, then schussed across a small flat with fine style, the hat clear in her mind's eye.

Just below the flat, Kurt, a giant Austrian ski instructor, was leading a jump class, showing six young hot-shots how to get air and land safely. He had stopped to explain something to them when out of nowhere came a cross between a bowling ball and a kamikaze with lip gloss, blowing right through the middle of his class. All seven skittles fell but the ball kept on.

Aunt Heather trilled, "Excuse me, gentlemen," without stopping or even turning her head.

Uncle Winston saw her careening onward ever onward without a hair out of place, and was filled with love and pride. He was laughing so hard he couldn't control his planks, and fell in a messy heap.

When he stopped sliding and flicked the snow out of his glasses, he looked up and saw the tiny figure, still in great form, descending like a homesick demon. She wasted no attention on the carnage behind her. She was keeping on keeping on, visualizing the finishing line and the hat.

As she flashed across the line, my uncle was still rolling in the snow powerless with laughter, but somehow looked at his watch: two minutes and forty-eight seconds.

Aunt Heather looked fabulous in that hat.

But I want an even better one. "The person who endures temptation will receive a crown of life, which God has promised to those who love him" (Jas 1:12).

One Bible writer said, "There's one thing I do. I forget those things which are behind, and I keep pushing forward to what is in front, and the prize of the high calling of God" (Paul, Phil 3:13–14).

So why look back? We're not going that way.